Miss Muffet or What Came After

by **MARILYN SINGER** • Pictures by **DAVID LITCHFIELD**

CLARION BOOKS | Houghton Mifflin Harcourt | Boston New York

Thanks to Steve Aronson, and Lynne Polvino

and the other good folks at Clarion. —M.S.

CLARION BOOKS
3 Park Avenue, New York, New York 10016.

Clarion Books is an imprint of Houghton Mifflin Harcourt Publishing Company.

www.hmhco.com

The illustrations in this book were done in mixed media.
The text was set in Quicksand.
Book design by Sharismar Rodriguez

Library of Congress Cataloging-in-Publication Data

Names: Singer, Marilyn, author. | Litchfield, David, illustrator.

Title: Miss Muffet, or what came after / by Marilyn Singer ; illustrated by David Litchfield.

Description: Boston ; New York : Clarion Books, an imprint of Houghton Mifflin Harcourt, [2016]

Summary: With the help of friendly spider Webster, aspiring violinists Patience Muffet and
Little Bo-Peep find personal fulfillment in the court of Old King Cole.

Identifiers: LCCN 2015028511 | ISBN 9780547905662 (hardback)

Subjects: | CYAC: Stories in rhyme. | Characters in literature—Fiction. | Violin—Fiction.
Musicians—Fiction. | Self-actualization (Psychology)—Fiction. | Spiders—Fiction.
BISAC: JUVENILE FICTION / Fairy Tales & Folklore / Adaptations. | JUVENILE NONFICTION /
Poetry / Humorous. | JUVENILE FICTION / Nursery Rhymes. | JUVENILE FICTION / Performing Arts / General.
JUVENILE FICTION / Animals / Insects, Spiders, etc. | JUVENILE FICTION / Imagination & Play.

Classification: LCC PZ8.3.S6154 Mi 2016 | DDC [E]—dc23
LC record available at http://lccn.loc.gov/2015028511

Manufactured in China
SCP 10 9 8 7 6 5 4 3 2 1
4500596659

To Jim and Cate —M.S.

To Katie and Ben —D.L.

Little Miss Muffet

Sat on a tuffet,

Eating her curds and whey;

Along came a spider,

Who sat down beside her,

And frightened Miss Muffet away.

The curtain opens on a lovely house with a proper English garden. There are two maids and a gardener, who form the chorus. They take on different costumes and occupations depending on the location. The narrator remains offstage.

Her given name was Patience.
Her schoolmates called her Pat.
In the garden on a stool
is where one day she sat.
What do we know about her?
Just this much, if you please:
She didn't care for spiders,
but she did love cottage cheese.

*Cottage cheese, cottage cheese,
she eats it every day.
Cottage, cottage, cottage cheese,
she calls it curds and whey.*

*In December or in June,
in a bowl, with a spoon.
Cottage cheese, cottage cheese.
Very tasty (slightly pasty),
or so we've heard her say!*

But though she kept it oh, so quiet,
there was more to Patience than her diet.
She had big dreams. She had ambition
to get her share of recognition.
She wanted to do something grand.
Her mother could not understand . . .

*Her mother couldn't understand
the sort of future Pat had planned
or her brand of grand ambition.
All girls should respect tradition!*

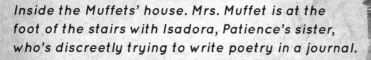

Inside the Muffets' house. Mrs. Muffet is at the foot of the stairs with Isadora, Patience's sister, who's discreetly trying to write poetry in a journal.

Where is that girl? Where can she be?
Why would she miss a shopping spree?
That dress she wears is out of style.
And, oh, my dear, her shoes are vile!
Patience tries my patience. Why can't she be like me?

Why can't she act proper, polite, and genteel?
Why won't she become every mother's ideal
          perfect little miss,
     who likes needlework, flowers, and fashion?
          Oh, why can't that girl share my passion?
               Now, wouldn't that be bliss!

Then there was Miss Muffet's dad—
a kindly gent, if slightly mad
for creatures with six legs or eight.
His bug collection was first-rate!
Mr. Muffet's big obsession
was to have in his possession
Aranea locutus, such a fabulous freak—
an exceptional spider that's able to speak!

A spider that can speak
in Latin or in Greek?
In English, Dutch, Chinese?
When can we meet him, please?

This creature's a *mole cricket*.
Yes, go ahead and pick it
up. It will not bite.
Observe the upper mandible.
An insect's understandable,
predictable, quite.
A beetle's wing, a silkworm's brain—
I find it easy to explain
their wherefore and their whence.
But children, well, I must admit,
I do not get them—not a whit.
They simply make no sense.

Take Patience—
how I've tried to guide her
to take delight in every spider,
in every insect in the garden.
But, sad to say, she doesn't care.
She always disappears somewhere . . .
Beg pardon? Oh, you've brought a tuffet.
Who ordered it? Ah, Mistress Muffet.
Money? Ah, yes. Will this amount do?
I hope this thing's mothproof. I'm joking. Adieu.

Where is Patience?
Where is she?
Did she climb the apple tree?
Did she go out horseback riding?
Where is Patience?
Where's she hiding?

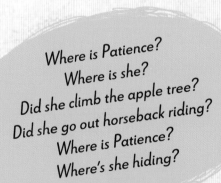

I do not care for ladies' stuff:
a feathered hat,
a lacy cuff.

I do not like arranging flowers,
sitting pretty,
wasting hours.

I haven't any interest
in a beehive
or a hornets' nest.

I *don't* need to identify
a beetle, gnat,
or damselfly.

Mother, Father, I'm not a riddle.
I simply want to play
the fiddle.

I'm not brainy or demure.
I plan someday
to go on tour!

She pulls a violin from the basket.

The violin's her only treasure.
Nothing else gives her such pleasure.
With bow in hand, she feels sublime,
but soon she loses track of time.
As Patience practices a tune,
Mama returns, a wee bit soon.

She's playing father's fiddle! Appalling and improper!
This will never, ever do. I simply have to stop her!
A spinet would be more than fine;
I think the organ's quite divine.
But a little miss with violin,
wrinkling her neck and chin,
wasting precious afternoons,
sawing raucous country tunes?
Dear heavens! I'll forbid it!
I'll declare that "Mother's spoken."
On second thought, I'll hide the thing
and simply say it's broken.

Poor Miss Muffet, disrespected.
Poor Miss Muffet, so dejected . . .

She takes the tuffet to the garden,
doesn't beg her mother's pardon,
sits there in the misty rain,
while the drizzle leaves a stain
on the fancy silk brocade.
Poor Miss Muffet feels betrayed.

She hears a small
voice right beside her.
Who could it be? Good grief!
The spider!

Good day, Two Legs.
Don't take fright.
You're not a tempting morsel;
hence, Webster will not bite.
Plus, I'm quite a fan of yours.
Your music's a delight.
I've often heard you in the shed,
where I hide from the light.
A silent spinner, catching flies,
I steer clear of your father,
who wants me for a prize.
What's wrong, Two Legs? Why the frown?
Why those downcast eyes?
Tell me, where's your music gone?
Maybe Webster can advise . . .

Is our Pat a wack kid
to talk with an arachnid,
a creature slightly ghoulish,
but one by no means foolish?
No! Though being sympathetic
is surely not genetic
in creatures of this ilk
(who capture prey with silk),
this spider has a heart
that grasps all kinds of art.
So this eensy music lover
moved quickly to discover
where that fine forbidden
violin was hidden.

And then what happened? Shall we guess?
They both were under so much stress.
One was avoiding capture; one following her dream.
It's a fact, they made a pact,
and off they went—a team.

JOURNAL

Yes, Mama, I've heard the news.
My little sister's run away.
She took issue with your views.
Yes, Mama, I've heard the news.
She slipped into her walking shoes.
She found her fiddle. She plans to play.
Yes, Mama, I've heard the news.
My little sister's run away.

I must say that I don't blame her.
How I wish I had the nerve!
Boredom finally overcame her.
I must say that I don't blame her.
Mama, you tried too hard to tame her.
A girl with ambition, talent, and verve.
I must say that I don't blame her.
How I wish I had the nerve!

And where is our Patience now?
Passing by field and plow,
stumbling by horse and cow.
She's got blisters.

Ow, ow, ow!

Webster tries to keep her spirits lifted,
but even he is not that gifted . . .

I'm hungry, footsore, also weary.
I will not let myself
get teary.

It must be nearly afternoon . . .
Say, isn't that
a fiddle tune?

Who's playing such a fine rendition?
I must meet this
grand musician.

Perhaps he plays upon the stage . . .
Look, it's a girl—
and of my age!

Strange as it may seem,
Pat is not the only girl
with a cherished dream.

I did not want to spend my life with sheep.
Their bleating was not music to my ears.
But still I did not plan to fall asleep,
and wake to face the worst of all my fears.
I rose to find them gone, each ewe and lamb.
Alack, the devil I must surely pay.
Alas, a rotten shepherdess I am
to let such foolish creatures go astray.
How many glens and meadows I did roam!
But not a single head nor tail did see.
Perhaps tomorrow they will go back home.
But they shall have to do so without me.
What future waits for me, Bo-Peep?
I have a fiddle. I'll earn my keep.

Patience thinks Bo-Peep could coach her.
But first of all, she must approach her.
The shepherdess is pleased to meet her.
Till Webster feels it's time to greet her.
Poor Little Bo turns white as chalk.
She's never heard a spider talk!
At first it's creepy and confusing.
But soon she finds he's quite amusing.

Yes, Bo-Peep, you're not losing your mind.
He really is witty and rather refined!

And off they travel . . .

On the road, traveling west,
our two misses need to rest.
They spy an empty caravan.
No sign of dame or gentleman.
Just a rooster, loudly warning.
Why's he crowing? It's not morning.

The Rooster tells the sad tale of the Montesquieus.

My mistress, she likes footin' it.
My master likes to bow and pluck.
Me, I like to strut my stuff
in front of gals that cluck.

Today they went a-picnicking
near several sheep and cows.
They had a meal; they danced and sang.
They soon began to drowse.

And as they napped, two chaps appeared
with bold but silent tread.
They found no gold nor jewels to steal.
They took the bow instead.

Their shoulders shook with muffled glee.
They found it oh, such sport.
I cock-a-doodled noisily,
their thievery to thwart.

My mistress woke and gave such chase
that off her slipper flew.
(It looks just like the other one—
a pretty shade of blue.)

My master, too, is in pursuit.
He's gone to who knows where.
Without a shoe and fiddlestick,
they do not have a prayer

of entering Old King Cole's court,
and they could use the work.
Now, get you gone to some safe place
where shameless thieves don't lurk.

How
wicked!

How
nasty!

How truly malicious!
To steal from a fiddler is
what I'd call vicious!

Let's teach them a lesson. It will be delicious!
Do you know any spies of the avian sort
who can locate those thieves, then return and report?

The rooter summons bird pals who can lead our travelers to the thieves.

Take that lane to reach them faster.
Can you save us from disaster,
fix those thieves, then find my master?
And my mistress all askew?
If so, then, thanks, and cock-a-doodle doo!

The thieves are sleeping under a tree. Patience and Bo-Peep climb it and let Webster dangle down.

You there, rogue! And you, barbarian!
I am not a vegetarian.
Prepare yourselves to meet your enemy.
You will find me rather venomy.

The thieves run off, leaving their loot.

Run, you cowards! Run, you fools!
What's their plunder? Several jewels,
a bit of silver, a stash of candy,
and there's the bow. Might come in handy.
Here are hard-boiled eggs and jellies,
bread and cheese to fill your bellies.
Here are pears and two meat pies,
currently attracting flies.
Later there'll be time to chatter.
You eat the former—I'll take the latter.
There's nothing like a bit of food
to brighten anybody's mood.

Brief change of scene (it's not a hassle):
a peek inside Old King Cole's castle.
A well-liked monarch, known as merry.
But today, alack, not very.

Even a merry old soul
gets a wee bit melancholy
at the preposterous folly
of all three of our fiddlers
struck down by bad fish!
We've got our pipe, we've got our bowl,
but how will we get our wish
for lively music that aids the digestion?
That is the question.
Can anyone offer a useful suggestion?

We will scour the castle!
We will scour the town!
We will travel the countryside,
first up, then down!

We'll search for new fiddlers,
and if we're in a bind
after searching for days
and no talent we find,

we will take a few lessons
and try our own hand . . .
No? Well, Your Majesty's wish
is, of course, our command!

Off they go to find a trio
that can play with spunk—*con brio*.
Drums won't work; a flute won't do.
The servants sense they're in a stew!

Every home and farm and bower,
how they search and how they scour.
Then in a glen, what's that they've heard?
It wasn't a tree frog, it wasn't a bird . . .

Play it again—that lovely air.
Show me again—my fingers go where?
Let's try it again—it's so nice to share . . .
Webster, you're singing! Well, I do declare!
We could be a trio instead of a pair!

The King's servants suddenly appear, startling the musicians.

Good day, little misses, your music's divine!
It's given me shivers right up my spine.
Now we have a reason to loudly rejoice . . .

Who was that singing in such a low voice?

Good news, little misses, this evening at nine,
right after dessert, you will both get to shine.
To the palace you're going! And we'll take you there!

What is that lurking in yon lass's hair?

Listen, you nitwits, has it not occurred
to your poor addled brains that we're missing a third?
The king gave an order and we MUST fulfill it!

Oh, no! It's a spider! Will somebody kill it?

He strikes the spider from Miss Muffet's head.
One more smack—and Webster's dead.

His life is hanging by a thread!
Oh, the shouts, the wails, the shrieks!

Suddenly, the spider speaks . . .

Hold your hand, sir! Do not strike me!
I think that you could get to like me.
I'm *Aranea locutus,* eloquent conveyer.
I know who could be your third fiddle player.
If you grant me your protection,
I'll point you in the right direction
to find him (and his missus), minus shoe and bow . . .

We've had the strangest day, *mon Dieu*!
We look like fools, *bien*, I've said it!
Oui, mes amis, so laugh *un peu*.

We've reached this well-to-do *milieu,*
but who sells bows or shoes on credit?
We've had the strangest day, *mon Dieu*!

Who's heard the name of Montesquieu?
Who gets the paper? Who has read it?
Oui, mes amis, so laugh *un peu*.

I dance; he plays. We're quite *fameux*.
(Though some reviews I've had to edit.)
We've had the strangest day, *mon Dieu*!

The servants appear with Miss Muffet, Bo-Peep, and Webster, interrupting Madame Montesquieu's villanelle.

The king needs what? Not *un*, not *deux* . . .
Fiddlers *trois*? What nonsense! Who spread it?
Oui, mes amis, so laugh *un peu*.

You swear it's true? Well, then, *adieu*!
A chance at court? I would not dread it.
We've had the strangest day, *mon Dieu*!
Oui, mes amis, so laugh *un peu*.

At the castle . . .
They arrive at the castle, a little bit flustered, just in time for pudding and custard.
We love pudding. We love custard. (Also Sunday roast with mustard!)
Everyone's a wee bit wary . . .
That band looks hopeless! That spider's hairy!

As soon as they begin to play,
all doubts are driven far away.
The music's superb; the dancing's fantastic . . .

*We're going to swoon! How that
spider can croon!
We swear we're not being sarcastic!*

The monarch's delighted, the first to admit
that Patience and friends are a definite hit!

We Fiddlers Three have gained great fame.
  (And Madame M.'s
    a household name.)

 People melt when Webster sings.
We're entertaining queens
    and kings!

My fondest wish has been surpassed.
My parents comprehend
    at last.

My sister's learning to write sonnets.
My mother's busy modeling
    bonnets.

My father plans to classify
our spider's daily
    food supply.

"Happily ever after" is such a fine cliché!
  It's even more delightful
      than a bowl of curds and whey!

Well, now you know about Miss Muffet,
who rose to such great glory.
As for Mary and her lamb—
well, that's another story . . .
Now, off to bed, where dreams take flight,
and friendly spiders sing good night!

THE END